For my parents, who always encouraged me to think outside the box and push my limits.
– Ellen

For my parents, who have always encouraged my immense curiosity about the world.
– Malgorzata

Originally published as *Monty's buitengewone dagje* in Belgium and the Netherlands by Clavis Uitgeverij, 2020
English translation from the Dutch by Clavis Publishing Inc., New York

Visit us on the Web at www.clavis-publishing.com.

Monty's Special Day written by Ellen DeLange and illustrated by Malgorzata Zajac

ISBN 978-1-60537-587-8

This book was printed in July 2020 by Grapso CZ, a.s., Pod Šternberkem 324, 763 02 Zlín, Czech Republic

First Edition
10 9 8 7 6 5 4 3 2 1

MONTY'S SPECIAL DAY

Ellen DeLange & Malgorzata Zajac

Clavis

NEW YORK

Monty is a typical donkey,
and he is having a typical donkey day.
Standing in the meadow, he chews
on heaps of grass, as he does every day.

CHOMP

CHOMP

CHOMP

CHOMP

And as he does every day, he goes on his morning and afternoon rounds. He checks on all his friends, taking time to stop at every corner of the yard.

Good morning, Mrs. Chicken. Good morning, Mr. Horse. Good afternoon, Woolly Sheep and Llama Llama.

All the animals in the meadow love Monty. He is always around, keeping them safe.

Yet while Monty is chewing the grass and looking after his friends, he often looks up to watch the birds fly overhead.

He wonders where they are going . . .

One morning, when Monty is doing his rounds,
he notices that the gate is open.
Loud honking noises overhead make him
look up—there are the geese again.

Monty has never left the farm before, but his curiosity
makes him walk through the gate and out of the meadow
to follow the birds.

Monty has to walk fast
to keep up with the geese,
and after a while he gets tired
and hungry.

He is happy when he sees
that the birds are perched
in a nearby tree. As he gets closer,
he sees them pecking at large red apples.

Monty thinks he'd like to try an apple too.
He eats one, and then another. Delicious!
Monty decides to save some for later.

Rested, and with a full belly,
Monty skips along the road
as he follows the birds.

Suddenly a very loud noise makes Monty jump . . .

ZOOFF . . . What a scare! Monty's heart is still pounding.

He decides that he needs to be more careful as he walks along the side of the road.

But due to the commotion, Monty has lost track of the birds.

"Where did they go?"

Splashing noises in the distance distract Monty,
and, curious, he follows a narrow path through
the tall reeds, which leads him to a river.
"There they are," he sighs.
The birds are swimming in the water. Some of them have
their heads in the water and are making funny noises.

BLUB **BLUB** **BLUB**
BLUB

"I would like to do that as well,"
Monty thinks, and he jumps
right in.

The birds fly off, and Monty swims across the river and climbs up the riverbank to continue his stroll. As he watches the birds in the sky, they seem to get smaller and smaller. "Phew, they are such fast fliers," Monty says to himself.

All of a sudden, something startles Monty and he stops in his tracks. What is that? Monty slowly gets closer and looks up at a GIANT animal. It looks a little bit like Monty, but it has a HUGE rack on its head, LONG, LONG legs, and almost no tail.

The moose does not seem to be disturbed by him at all and continues eating juicy berries from the bushes.

"I think I'll try that too," Monty decides, and side by side Monty and the moose pick away at the sweet fruit.

Monty walks on and arrives at the foot
of the hill, where he spots small animals
with fluffy tails who are frantically
running around, gathering seeds and nuts.

Monty looks at the shenanigans
of the playful, rowdy squirrels
and thinks, "that's not for me at all . . ."

A strange noise catches his attention.
It becomes louder and louder . . .

THUD!

A BIG tree falls on the ground next to Monty.
Startled, he jumps up and runs as fast as he can
up the hill, away from the busy beavers.

When he arrives at the top, he is out of breath and exhausted.
Monty is lying down to rest for a little while, wondering
where to go next, when he hears the familiar honking
of birds flying overhead.

He looks in the direction in which the birds were flying.

"Wait, isn't that my meadow in the distance?"

Monty jumps up and runs down the hill.

He knows exactly where to go . . .

The farm animals are waiting for Monty at the gate.
They wondered where he had gone and hope
he is okay. It is going to be dark soon.

When they see Monty running down the hill, they are very happy. "Where have you been, Monty?" they ask. "How was your day? We want to hear all about it!"

The animals gather around Monty as he shares the apples, nuts, and berries he has carried home. They are very excited to hear how Monty's typical donkey day turned into a very special donkey day.
"My day was full of adventure," he said.
"Now I know that the birds also make a daily round and go home at the end of the day."

"It's great to go places," he tells his friends.
"But it's even better to come back home."
And then Monty falls into a deep sleep.

ZzZ...